P9-DEL-913

Floppy Teddy Bear

By PATRICIA LILLIE

Pictures by KAREN LEE BAKER

Greenwillow Books, New York

Watercolor paints were used for the full-color art. The text type is Goudy.

Printed in Hong Kong by Wing King Tong
First Edition 10 9 8 7 6 5 4 3 2 1

Library of Congress Cataloging-in-Publication Data
Lillie, Patricia.
Floppy teddy bear / by Patricia Lillie; pictures by Karen Lee Baker.
p. cm.
Summary: A new teddy bear causes dissension within a family.
ISBN 0-688-12570-0
[1. Teddy bears—Fiction 2. Sisters—Fiction.]
I. Baker, Karen (date), ill. II. Title.
PZ7.L632Fl 1995 [E]—dc20
93-26516 CIP AC

For Ray and Vera,
Tammy and Shannon,
JessiAnn and Erin
—P. L.

For my sisters,
Amy and Cheryl
—K. L. B.

Mama, she bought me a floppy teddy bear,
Mama, she bought me a floppy teddy bear,
Curly brown fur and two black eyes.

Mama, she bought me a floppy teddy bear.

Me, I love my floppy teddy bear,
Me, I love my floppy teddy bear,
Curly brown fur and two black eyes,
A squishy-squashy belly and a red bow tie.

Me, I love my floppy teddy bear.

Sister, she wants my floppy teddy bear,
Sister, she wants my floppy teddy bear,
Curly brown fur and two black eyes,
A squishy-squashy belly and a red bow tie,
Two soft ears and a round black nose.

No, she cannot have my floppy teddy bear!

Sister, she took my floppy teddy bear,
Sister, she took my floppy teddy bear,
Took him in the kitchen to feed him lunch.

Sister, she took my floppy teddy bear.

Me, I love my floppy teddy bear,
Me, I love my floppy teddy bear,
Peanut butter in his fur and two black eyes,
A squishy-squashy belly and jelly on his tie,
Two soft ears and a round black nose.

Me, I love my floppy teddy bear.

Sister, she took my floppy teddy bear,
Sister, she took my floppy teddy bear,
Took him outside to play with the dog.

Sister, she took my floppy teddy bear.

Me, I love my floppy teddy bear,
Me, I love my floppy teddy bear,
Peanut butter in his fur and one black eye,
A squishy-squashy belly and jelly on his tie,
Two torn ears and a hole in his nose.

Me, I love my floppy teddy bear.

Sister, she took my floppy teddy bear,
Sister, she took my floppy teddy bear,
Put him in the sink and left him there.

Sister, she took my floppy teddy bear.

Me, I love my soggy teddy bear,
Me, I love my soggy teddy bear,
Peanut butter in his fur and one black eye,
A splishy-splashy belly and jelly on his tie,
Two torn ears and a hole in his nose.

Me, I love my soggy teddy bear.

Mama, she fixed my soggy teddy bear,
Mama, she fixed my soggy teddy bear,
Peanut butter in his fur and one black eye,
A splishy-splashy belly and jelly on his tie,
Two torn ears and a hole in his nose.

Mama, she fixed my soggy teddy bear.

Me, I love my floppy teddy bear,
Me, I love my floppy teddy bear,
Curly brown fur and two black eyes,
A squishy-squashy belly and a red bow tie,
Two soft ears and a round black nose.

Me, I love my floppy teddy bear.

Sister, she wants my floppy teddy bear,
Sister, she wants my floppy teddy bear.
She may be my sister, but I don't care,
She

cannot,

cannot,

cannot,

cannot

have my

floppy teddy bear!

Mama and me, we went to the store,
Mama and me, we went to the store,
Didn't take long, knew what we were looking for.

Mama and me, we went to the store.

Sister, she loves her floppy teddy bear,
Sister, she loves her floppy teddy bear,
Curly black fur and two brown eyes,
A squishy-squashy belly and a yellow bow tie,
Two soft ears and a round black nose.

Sister, she loves her floppy teddy bear,

Sister, she loves her floppy teddy bear!